GAME OVER,
SUPER RABBIT BOY!

READ MORE
PRESS START!
BOOKS!

MORE BOOKS COMING SOON!

PRESS START!

GAME OVER, SUPER RABBIT BOY!

THOMAS FLINTHAM

BRANCHES

SCHOLASTIC INC.

FOR JACK

Library of Congress Cataloging-in-Publication Data
Flintham, Thomas, author, illustrator.
Game over, Super Rabbit Boy! / by Thomas Flintham.
First edition. | New York : Branches/Scholastic Inc., 2017.

Series: Press Start! Summary: When King Viking and his evil robot army attack Animal Town, and kidnap Singing
Dog, it is up to Super Rabbit Boy, with some help from Sunny and his video game console, to save the day
Identifiers: LCCN 2016028028 (print) LCCN 2016030058 (ebook) ISBN 9781338034714 (digest pbk.)
ISBN 9781338034721 (jacketed library binding) | ISBN 9781338035254 (e-Book)
Subjects: LCSH: Superheroes—Juvenile fiction. | Supervillains—Juvenile
fiction. | Animals—Juvenile fiction. | Video games—Juvenile fiction.

CYAC: Superheroes—Fiction. | Supervillains—Fiction. Animals—Fiction. Video games--Fiction.
Classification: LCC PZ7.1.F585 Gam 2017 (print) | LCC PZ7.1.F585 (ebook)

DDC [E]—dc23
LC record available at https://lccn.loc.gov/2016028028

ISBN 978-1-338-03472-1 (hardcover) / ISBN 978-1-338-03471-4 (paperback)

18 17 16 15 14   20 21

Printed in China   62
First edition, January 2017
Edited by Celia Lee
Book design by Maeve Norton

TABLE OF CONTENTS

This is Animal Town.

It is a peaceful town full of happy animal friends. The townspeople have fun all the time. They play games. They dance. They have a party every day.

This is Singing Dog. He lives in Animal
Town. He loves happiness. He loves fun.
And he loves to make other people happy.
Everyone has fun with Singing Dog. Singing
Dog really knows how to be happy!

Singing Dog

This is King Viking. He lives in Boom Boom Factory high up on Mount Boom. He does not like happiness. He does not like fun. And he really does not like other people who are happy and fun. Not one bit.

King Viking

King Viking can't stand the fun going on in Animal Town. He has never danced. He has never played games. He has only ever been mean! So he has come up with a No-Fun Plan.

Ha! Ha! Ha! I'll put a stop to happiness once and for all!

NO-FUN PLAN

- BUILD ROBOT ARMY.

- STEAL SINGING DOG.

- USE ROBOTS TO SPREAD NO FUN THROUGHOUT THE LAND.

King Viking and his Robot Army travel across the land. They travel from Boom Boom Factory all the way to Animal Town.

The townspeople run away in fear when they see King Viking. Everyone knows he is mean and horrible. He brings trouble with him everywhere.

Oh no! Singing Dog is too busy singing
and dancing. He doesn't see King Viking and
his Robot Army!

King Viking rushes back to Boom Boom Factory. But he leaves his robots behind.

3 SUPER RABBIT BOY!

Simon the Hedgehog runs as fast as his legs can carry him. He runs all the way to Carrot Castle.

Help! Help! Eek! Eek! Help! Help! Eek! Eek!

Simon?

Then the greatest hero of all time steps out of the castle: Super Rabbit Boy!

Flashback . . .

WHEN HE WAS ONLY A BABY, RABBIT BOY CRAWLED TO THE WOODS TO FIND SOMETHING TO EAT.

BUT HE FELL THROUGH A HOLE INTO A VERY SPECIAL BONUS MAZE LEVEL.

AFTER A LONG, HUNGRY SEARCH, RABBIT BOY FOUND A SHINY SUPER CARROT IN THE CENTER OF THE MAZE. IT LOOKED VERY TASTY. RABBIT BOY GULPED IT UP IN ONE BITE!

Crunch, crunch, nom, nom, yum, yum!

BUT IT WAS NO ORDINARY CARROT. IT WAS A SUPER MAGICAL CARROT!

FROM THAT DAY FORWARD, WHENEVER RABBIT BOY ATE A SUPER MAGICAL CARROT, HE COULD JUMP REALLY HIGH . . .

. . . AND RUN REALLY, REALLY FAST! (EVEN FASTER THAN SIMON THE HEDGEHOG!)

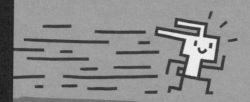

HE WAS THE STRONGEST AND BRAVEST ANIMAL IN ANIMAL TOWN. RABBIT BOY SWORE TO ALWAYS USE HIS SPECIAL POWERS FOR GOOD. HE BECAME KNOWN TO EVERYONE AS **SUPER** RABBIT BOY!

Simon the Hedgehog tells Super Rabbit
Boy what happened. He tells him how King
Viking and his Robot Army stormed the
town and kidnapped poor Singing Dog.

Super Rabbit Boy is angry.

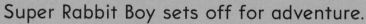

Super Rabbit Boy sets off for adventure.

There are six levels between Super Rabbit Boy's home and the end of his adventure.

LEVEL 1: ANIMAL TOWN
LEVEL 2: SPLISH SPLASH SEA
LEVEL 3: SANDSTORM DESERT
LEVEL 4: CLOUDY HILLS
LEVEL 5: MOUNT BOOM
LEVEL 6: BOOM BOOM FACTORY

Each level is harder than the one before. Can Super Rabbit Boy beat them all?

Super Rabbit Boy springs into action on Level 1.

He finds some carrots to power up.

He hops from platform to platform.

And he jumps on King Viking's robots along the way. Jumping stops the robots!

Super Rabbit Boy completed the level!

Super Rabbit Boy eats a couple of carrots before jumping into the water.

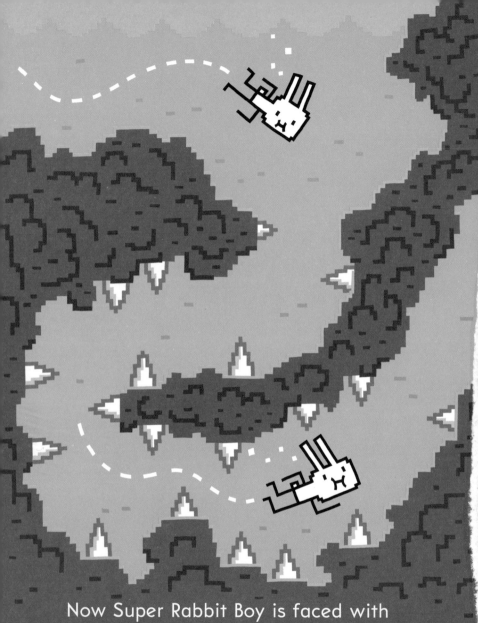

Now Super Rabbit Boy is faced with many new dangers. He swims through small tunnels covered in spikes.

He dodges King Viking's Robo-Crabs and Robo-Fish as they try to grab and bite him.

He is getting tired, and he's running out of carrot power. Finally, the Exit is just ahead. Super Rabbit Boy is almost there when suddenly . . .

A GIANT Robo-Fish has gobbled up Super Rabbit Boy! **Oh no!**

2 LIVES LEFT!

Sigh. Let's go, Super Rabbit Boy!

Super Rabbit Boy is back at the beginning of Level 2. He is a little confused.

Super Rabbit Boy swims ahead through the level. But everything feels familiar.

None of the traps and tricks surprise him.
He seems to always know which way to go,
and which tunnels to take.

Ha! Ha! You can't catch me!

He is ready for every Robo-Crab and every
Robo-Fish.

Even the Giant Robo-Fish is no surprise.

Super Rabbit Boy swims to the Exit.

Hooray! Level 2 is finished!

LEVEL 3: SANDSTORM DESERT

Super Rabbit Boy sees a large, sandy desert as far as he can see. Super Rabbit Boy spots the Exit in the distance.

I can see the Exit already! This is going to be easy!

Super Rabbit Boy lands on the sand and starts running toward the Exit.

Poor Super Rabbit Boy! **Oh no!**

Super Rabbit Boy is back at the beginning of Level 3. He's a little confused. Everything looks familiar. But he remembers something important.

Super Rabbit Boy jumps into action once again. This time, he hops all the way!

He hops from rock to rock.

He hops across the sand.

He hops on any Robo-Lizards that he
finds in the desert.

Soon Super Rabbit Boy is almost at the Exit. He just needs to pass one last stretch of desert. The problem is it's full of swimming, munching, crunching, giant Robo-Snakes!

Super Rabbit Boy does not like snakes.
But he is very brave. He jumps straight
ahead. The Robo-Snakes jump out at him. He
dodges the first Robo-Snake.

He hops right past the second Robo-Snake.

He leaps quickly between the third and
fourth Robo-Snakes.

And he bounces straight into the mouth
of the fifth and final Robo-Snake!

LEVEL 3: SANDSTORM DESERT

Super Rabbit Boy is back at the beginning of Level 3. He is confused. But he quickly hops through the level toward the Robo-Snakes. Before Super Rabbit Boy faces the Robo-Snakes again, he sees a ledge.

Super Rabbit Boy jumps down. It's an entrance to a secret tunnel!

He runs through the tunnel.

Finally he is back out in the sunlight and right next to the Exit! The Robo-Snakes hiss as he waves good-bye.

With no lives left, Super Rabbit Boy enters Cloudy Hills.

LEVEL 4: CLOUDY HILLS

The platforms lead him up into the sky to Mount Boom. Boom Boom Factory sits at the very top of Mount Boom.

Super Rabbit Boy sees carrots. The more carrots he eats, the more super rabbit power he has. The more power he has, the higher he can jump.

He jumps from hill to platform.

From platform to hill.
Higher and higher.

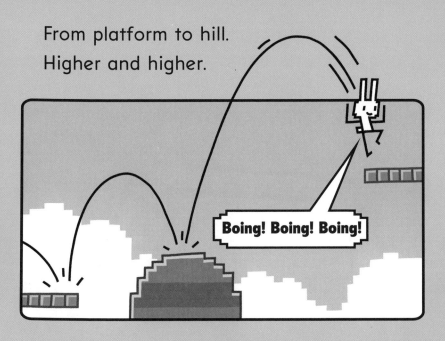

Super Rabbit Boy is almost at the end of the level. He just has to make it across one last very, very, **VERY** big gap.

Luckily, he can jump really, really, **REALLY** high because of all the carrots he has eaten. He leaps over the very, very, **VERY** big gap . . . straight through the Exit.

UH-OH

LEVEL 5: MOUNT BOOM

Mount Boom is a very scary place. Super Rabbit Boy has no more lives left. But he is very, **VERY** brave! He leaps into action.

He jumps across lakes of lava!

He dodges fireballs!

He jumps from robot to robot!

Suddenly two giant robots jump out right in front of Super Rabbit Boy!

Robo-Basher Brother 1 swings his fist from the left. Super Rabbit Boy quickly hops out of the way.

Super Rabbit Boy lands in front of Robo-Basher Brother 2 who is already swinging his fist in from the right! He leaps once again, narrowly missing the giant robot's powerful punch.

He has avoided both punches.

Oh bloop! That was close!

But this time, Super Rabbit Boy lands right between the two robot brothers. They are swinging their fists at him from both directions!

9 IF AT FIRST. . .

GAME START!

Super Rabbit Boy is back at Carrot Castle with Simon the Hedgehog.

Be careful, Super Rabbit Boy! King Viking's robots are everywhere.

Um, don't worry, Simon. Super Rabbit Boy is on the way. Again?

Super Rabbit Boy speeds through each level.
He swims past the Robo-Fish!

He runs through the secret tunnel!

He leaps over the very, very, **VERY** big gap!

Soon Super Rabbit Boy is back in front of the Robo-Basher Brothers in Level 5. He hops, runs, and leaps as hard as he can, but they beat him again . . .

and again . . .

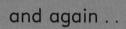

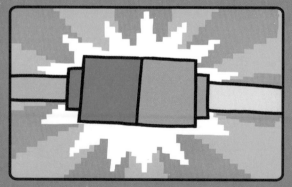

and again.

No matter how hard he tries, it always ends in . . .

Once again Super Rabbit Boy faces the Robo-Basher Brothers. But this time is different.

Super Rabbit Boy dodges every punch. He remembers their punching pattern! First he dodges a punch from the left, then from the right.

And with a quick double hop onto both robots' heads . . .

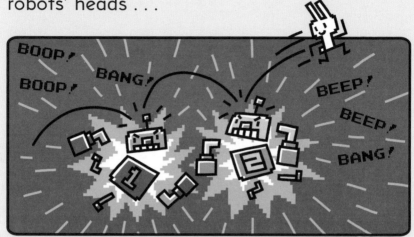

Super Rabbit Boy beats them at last! He is ready to move on to the final level.

LEVEL 6: BOOM BOOM FACTORY

Now Super Rabbit Boy enters the final level.
Inside the factory, it is very dark and scary!
Tunnels and paths lead in every direction.

Which way should I go?

Super Rabbit Boy goes from tunnel to tunnel and through door after door. But there is no sign of King Viking or Singing Dog.

This place is a maze! Where are they? Wait! What's that noise?

Super Rabbit Boy can hear a familiar sound coming down one of the tunnels. He heads toward it. The closer he gets, the louder the sound gets.

Right away, he dashes through the maze toward the source of the sound.

At long last, Super Rabbit Boy has found Singing Dog . . .

. . . with a dancing, smiling, and laughing King Viking?

Suddenly, King Viking spots Super Rabbit Boy!
He stops dancing and Super Rabbit Boy laughs.

Super Rabbit Boy has had enough of King Viking and his robots. He swam through traps, escaped Robo-Snakes, survived lava, and beat an entire army of super-mean robots. He is ready to finish this adventure once and for all.

He leaps in the air and hops on the head
of King Viking's Mega Robo-Viking Armor once.

Then twice.

Then three times.

The armor explodes with a big blast! King Viking is flung right through the roof of Boom Boom Factory!

Back in Animal Town, there is a big
party to thank Super Rabbit Boy for saving
Singing Dog. Singing Dog sings better than
ever and everyone has lots and lots and
LOTS of FUN!

Super Rabbit Boy has brought happiness
back to Animal Town!